3.9

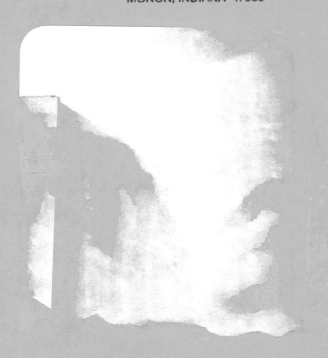

3.9

JAKE JOHNSON

The Story of a Mule

by TRES SEYMOUR
pictures by MARSHA GRAY CARRINGTON

A DK INK BOOK
DK PUBLISHING, INC.

A *Richard Jackson* Book

DK Publishing, Inc.
95 Madison Avenue
New York, New York 10016

Visit us on the World Wide Web at http://www.dk.com

Library of Congress Cataloging-in-Publication Data
Seymour, Tres.
Jake Johnson: the story of a mule / by Tres Seymour; illustrated by Marsha Gray Carrington. — 1st ed.
p.   cm.
"A Richard Jackson book."
Summary: Farmer Puckett's custom of hauling a wagonload of fireworks to the fairgrounds
for the Independence Day Social is endangered when his stubborn mule Jake Johnson refuses to move.
ISBN 0-7894-2563-7
[1. Mules—Fiction.   2. Obstinacy—Fiction.   3. Fireworks—Fiction.   4. Fourth of July—Fiction.]
I. Carrington, Marsha Gray, ill.   II. Title.
PZ7.S5253Jak   1998   [E]—dc21   98-7373   CIP   AC

Book design by Jennifer Browne
The illustrations for this book were painted in acrylic on board.
The text of this book is set in 16 point Novarese.
Printed and bound in U.S.A.

First Edition, 1999

2   4   6   8   10   9   7   5   3   1

For John,
who is, at heart, a mule-skinner.
—T.S.

For my family and friends.
Special thanks to Barbara, Dick, and Jane.
—M.G.C.

Farmer Puckett had a great big wagon. Folks in town used to ask him to haul fireworks to the fairgrounds for the Independence Day Social. He would deck his wagon out in red, white, and blue crepe paper and go rolling into town whistling "Yankee Doodle." Mrs. Puckett rode beside him on the buckboard wearing her fancy Fourth of July hat, proud as a banty rooster.

That is, they *used* to.

One year, about a month before the Social, Farmer Puckett took a notion that he needed a new mule to pull his wagon. So he went to the stockyard and bought himself a *hu-mon-gous* mule named Jake Johnson.

Trouble was, when Jake Johnson got to Farmer Puckett's yard, the mule liked the place so much he sat down.

And he would not get up.

Now you'd think a mule could only weigh so much. But Farmer Puckett pulled for all he was worth, and pushed for all he was worth, and he still couldn't lift up that mule, not even the bottom half.

Farmer Puckett tried to raise Jake Johnson up with a plank, but it splintered like a cheap school pencil.

"You ought to use what's left of your plank to knock some sense into that mule," said Mrs. Puckett.

"Good glory," said Mr. Puckett. "I wouldn't want to hurt the poor, sweet animal."

"Poor, sweet animal my foot," said Mrs. Puckett. But they put the plank away.

It wasn't long before Jake Johnson took a powerful hunger. He hollered out for some supper. *"HAAAAWWWWWWW!"*

"Don't you feed him," said Mrs. Puckett from the kitchen doorway. "He'll get up if he gets hungry enough."

Jake Johnson didn't get up. He just hollered,
"HAAAAWWWWWWW!
    HAAAAWWWWWWW!
        HAAAAWWWWWWW!" so loud that
Mrs. Puckett's best dishes fell to pieces on her kitchen floor.

"Good glory," said Farmer Puckett. "Best not starve that poor, sweet animal. He'll whittle away to nothing."

"Poor, sweet animal my hind leg," muttered Mrs. Puckett, picking up the shards. The farmer brought Jake Johnson a forkful of hay.

Later on Jake Johnson took a powerful thirst. He hollered out to Farmer Puckett, *"HAAAAWWWWWWW!"* and licked his big, soft, whiskery lips.

"Don't you give him a drop," said Mrs. Puckett from the kitchen window. "He'll get up if he gets thirsty enough."

Jake Johnson didn't get up. He just got thirstier and thirstier. At last Jake Johnson sniffed the ground, stamped his sharp hoof into the turf, and broke the water line to the house.

Then he had a good drink.

"Good glory," said Farmer Puckett. "If we didn't mistreat that poor, sweet animal, we wouldn't have these troubles."

"Poor, sweet animal my big toe," said Mrs. Puckett with dish suds all over her hands.

Farmer Puckett tried everything he could think of to make Jake Johnson move. He tried honking horns and waving carrots on sticks and prodding with pitchforks, but try as he might, he could not get the mule to move.

And so Jake Johnson sat.
And the hours went by...
and the days...
and the weeks...

JULY

And Jake Johnson never moved,
right up to the Fourth of July.

Now Farmer Puckett had done given up on Jake Johnson and had begun to think of him sort of like a big, hairy rock in the yard. He'd also given up on ever getting the fireworks to the fairgrounds. In fact, he'd took on a case of the mopes, thinking that nobody in town would ever ask him to haul the fireworks again.

Mrs. Puckett had not given up. She had a brand-new Fourth of July hat with the tag still on, and she meant to ride that cart of fireworks into town. No fool mule was going to get in her way.

She sat in her kitchen, steaming hotter than the coffeepot on the wood stove. As she watched the flames lick around the bottom of the pot, she got an idea, swift and sharp.

"There's just one thing we haven't tried," she said, jumping up.

She made Farmer Puckett put the fireworks in his wagon and hitch it to the mule (who remained seated). Then she made a big pile of sticks, hay, and old copies of the *County News-Herald* all around Jake Johnson's haunches.

"If this don't move you," Mrs. Puckett said into the mule's long ear, "I don't know what will." Then, striking a match, she lit a fire under Jake Johnson's rump and leaped onto the seat of the wagon.

Jake Johnson moved.

He rose, seemed to stretch, and then, pulling the wagon, walked four paces forward until the wagon stood right over the fire.

Then Jake Johnson sat down again.

As the fingers of flame reached up and licked the fancy wagon bed, Farmer Puckett hollered, "Good glory!"

Mrs. Puckett said, "That fool mule!"

Then the fuses on the load of fireworks began to spark.

When the first sparkler went *FIZZZZ!* Jake Johnson got bug-eyed.

When the first
Roman candle went
WHOOOOSH! WHOOOOSH!
Jake Johnson went *"SNORT!"*

And when the first flaming firecrackers
went *CRACK! CRACK! CRACK-CRACK!*
Jake Johnson went *"HAAAAWWWWWW!"*
and shot down the dirt road like a bottle rocket,
headed straight for town, with Mrs. Puckett clinging
to the buckboard and hollering to save her life.

Farmer Puckett sighed and started down the road after them, on foot. He found Mrs. Puckett's brand-new Fourth of July hat on the road halfway there. It was a little singed, but otherwise in pretty good shape.

For years after that, everybody in town would say that was the best-lit-up Independence Day Social there ever was.

But Mrs. Puckett never rode that wagon again, and Jake Johnson . . .

Well, he sat down on the courthouse lawn...
and I reckon he's still there.